The Troublesome Tales of Sir Trober

by

Georgie and Robbie Jones

New Generation Publishing

The Knights of the Idrim

A long time ago, by the sea, stood a great city called Idris. It was a large city with the biggest harbour in all the lands, filled with ships that sailed to all corners of the world. In the centre of the city was a steep green hill, and at the top of the hill was the castle. Here lived the Lady of Idris and her family, who ruled the city. Also living at the castle, were the 7 knights of the Idrim, the greatest knights in all the Kingdom. It was their job to protect the castle, the city and the harbour from any danger. The leader of the knights was Sir Ardnax the Dragonheart. His second in command was Sir Liw and the other five were Sir Vic, Sir Sej, Sir Anni Groeg, Sir Narf and finally Sir Trober. Although the knights were all brave and strong, many troublesome tales are told of their adventures, most of which involve Sir Trober…

The tales in this book:

IDRIS

1. Sir Trober the Cake Maker

Once upon a time, Sir Trober was feeling hungry. When he found that Sir Vic had finished all the cake in the knight's quarters, he went to the kitchens, but he still could not find any cake anywhere. The very busy cook who was more than a little fed up of knights taking food from his kitchen, told him to make his own.

'Fine then, I will,' said Sir Trober. 'First of all I will need some ingredients though…' The Cook quickly gave him a list of ingredients and told him to go away. Sir Trober thought very carefully about each of the items on the list, before heading out to find them all.

First of all he went to the Mill. 'I need some flour!' he said to the Miller. 'I'm making a cake. Quick quick!'

Now the Miller was very busy grinding flour for everyone living in the castle, and he thought that Sir Trober was being very rude. Suddenly he had an idea. He picked up a small bag containing dust that he had swept up from the floor that morning, 'Here you go,' he said to Sir Trober.

'Good good,' said Sir Trober, and he was so excited to make his cake that he left without even saying thank you!

The Miller scratched his head thoughtfully, before quickly writing 3 letters, which he then gave to his fastest boy to deliver around the castle grounds.

Next Sir Trober went to get some milk and butter from the dairy. 'I need some milk and butter for the cake I'm making!' he said loudly as he burst through the door. The poor Dairy Maid was in the middle of the morning milking, and had only just put down the two pails she

was carrying to read a letter she had got from the Miller, when Sir Trober had burst in. 'Quick quick!' he shouted.

'One moment Sir,' the Dairy Maid said, putting the letter in her pocket. Thinking quickly, she went through a door into the next room which the castle painter had been repainting white. She poured some of the white paint into a milk pail, and then went through another door into the cheese and butter making room. Here

2

she picked up a block of cheese that had spent too long in the sun. Wrapping the melting block of cheese in paper, she returned to Sir Trober, and handed him the pail of white paint and the package. 'There you go Sir,' she said politely with a bright smile.

Sir Trober was so excited about making his cake, that all he said was 'good good!' and left without even saying thank you, nearly sloshing the paint from the milk pail.

The dairy maid giggled to herself before returning to finish milking the row of cows.

After the dairy, Sir Trober hurried to the chicken houses. 'I need some eggs to make a cake!' he said loudly to the boy who looked after the hens. The boy quickly scrunched up the letter he had just

been reading, and smiled at Sir Trober. 'Quick quick!' said Sir Trober loudly, eager to get on with making his cake.

'One moment Sir,' said the boy as he turned to the basket of eggs he had just collected. 'I  have some better eggs inside.'

He carried the egg basket inside, being careful not to drop any. He then picked up the three eggs he had found the day before that the hens had laid in a bush (instead of in the hen house). The boy did not know how long the eggs had been in this bush, but it could have been a few weeks given that they had a funny white colour to them, and the boy thought they might be rotten.

'Here we are Sir!' he said to Trober, as he gave him the eggs in a small basket.

'Good good!' said Sir Trober as he left, again, without even saying thank you.

The boy who looked after the hens, clapped his hands with glee, before returning to collect the rest of the eggs.

Finally Sir Trober hurried back to the kitchens, 'I need some sugar to make a cake!' he said loudly to the grumpy man who looked after the kitchen stores. The grumpy man looked up grumpily from the letter in his hands, and frowned at Sir Trober down his long nose. 'One moment Sir,' he said slowly, before heading into the store room. He tapped his chin thoughtfully, before taking a small paper bag and filling it with salt. 'Here we are Sir!' he said to Sir Trober, handing him the bag.

'Good good!' said Sir Trober, and rushed off to the kitchen, without even saying thank you.

'Hmmm,' said the grumpy man.

Sir Trober put all the ingredients in a bowl and mixed them together. The Cook at first tried to keep an eye on what he was doing, but soon the smell got too bad, and everyone in the kitchens kept their distance from the corner where Sir Trober was working. Sir Trober didn't seem to notice the smell. Having never made a cake before, he thought it must be normal. Finally, he put the cake in a tin in the oven, and strolled off out of the kitchen for a nap whilst the cake cooked; it had after all been a most tiring morning.

The kitchen workers tried to ignore the smell of rotten eggs and paint that came from the oven, but it only got worse and worse. The servant girls and boys all tied their handkerchiefs around their noses, and the Cook changed the menu for

dinner that evening to reduce the amount of work in the kitchen.

Minutes passed and still Sir Trober did not return. 20 minutes, 30 minutes passed. At 40 minutes, the Miller, the Dairy Maid and the boy who looked after the chickens came to the kitchen, each holding a number of packages, and spoke quickly and quietly to the Cook, who at first looked angry, but then smiled and nodded. The three left. 50 minutes, 55 minutes passed. Finally after a full hour had passed Sir Trober came running into the kitchen, and pulled his cake from the oven, forgetting to use a cloth and burning his fingers. Whilst putting them under the cold tap, he stared at the cake he had made. It was a black mess, which looked more like a pool of burned mud than anything worth eating. Sir Trober wasn't even sure he would be able to cut it, let alone eat it. There was also a rotten smelling smoke coming from the centre of the cake. As he was standing there, the Cook came up, mouth covered by a handkerchief,

and looked over Sir Trober's shoulder. 'What did I miss?' asked Sir Trober sadly. 'I put in everything you said.'

'I do believe you forgot your 'pleases' and 'thank yous,' ' said the Cook.

Sir Trober felt very bad then. 'I'm sorry,' he said to the Cook.

'Very good,' said the Cook, 'But I think your apologies are required elsewhere. In fact, I have an idea...'

Sir Trober and the Cook then worked together to make a cake. This time the smell when it was cooking brought all the servant girls and boys back to the kitchens, and they quickly got on with preparing dinner. When the Cook told Sir Trober to remove the cake from the oven, it was a beautiful golden brown. They left it to cool, and Sir Trober guarded it from any hungry kitchen workers, whilst the Cook made butter icing. Finally the Cook iced the cake with a sweep of a knife and it was finished!

But did they eat it then and there? No they most certainly did not. Sir Trober cut the cake up into many slices. He gave one to the Miller, one to the Dairy Maid, and one to the boy who looked after the chickens. He even gave a piece to the grumpy man who looked after the kitchen stores.

The rest he gave to the workers in the kitchen, and the very last piece he gave to the Cook. 'Thank you for helping me,' he said.

'You can have the piece of cake.' said the Cook, 'as long as you come back and help us sometimes! Now I've taken the time to teach you, you should make yourself useful!'

And so in this way, Sir Trober learned to be more polite, to listen and learn from others, and also to become the resident birthday cake maker in the castle.

2. Sir Trober and the Dark Knight

Once upon a time, Sir Trober was riding through the woods near the city. He was supposed to be on patrol duty with Sir Narf, but Sir Narf had been called to help Sir Liw with a very important secret task, and so Trober was all by himself. 'It had not been a good day,' thought Trober to himself. He was just getting close to the cross roads where he would turn to head back to the castle when he heard the sound of horse hooves ahead of him. Trober slowed his horse down and continued more slowly. He didn't normally meet any other horses on the road. As he turned the next corner however, he saw a knight standing by a black horse at the crossroads, letting the horse drink from the water pump. He was wearing dark old armour, and a dark torn cloak and on his head he wore a dented helmet with the visor down, and Trober did not

7

recognise him one bit. 'You there,' he called out, not feeling very brave at all, but trying to sound bold. 'What is your name and what brings you to Idris?'

The Dark Knight turned to face him, 'I would ask you the same thing,' he said.

'I am Sir Trober of the Idrim,' said Sir Trober loudly, 'Now your turn.'

The Dark Knight paused for a bit. 'No,' he said. 'I will not give you my name.'

Sir Trober was feeling nervous now. This wasn't what was supposed to happen when he questioned people... 'Well then,' he said, 'Well you shall have to come with me back to the castle for questioning.' and he drew his sword.

The Dark Knight just stared at him, and Trober could just about see his dark eyes through the visor of his helm.

'How about we make a deal?' the Dark Knight said, just when Trober was about to take a deep breath and shout.

'What sort of a deal?' asked Trober, hoping it was the kind of deal where the Knight came with him to make a deal with more important people at the castle, who were the kind of people better at making deals than Trober was.

'How about,' said the Dark Knight, 'We fight here and now to decide if you'll let me go.'

'Won't we have to do that anyway?' said Trober, confused.

'Ah but in my deal,' the Dark Knight said, climbing up onto his horse, 'No one gets hurt. The first man to fall off his horse loses.

I win, you have to let me go. You win, I'll come with you.'

Trober thought very carefully. He thought about the Knight's old armour, and dented helmet. It wasn't anywhere near as good as Trober's shiny armour and shield…but could he definitely beat him?

The Dark Knight sighed, 'It is as I thought,' he said, 'The lazy knight is too scared to fight me. He thinks he can be beaten by a poor homeless knight, and would rather try and fight me to come with him and me run off so that he can run home to cry to the other knights…'

'I am not scared!' said Trober. 'I could beat you easily!'

'Deal?' said the Dark Knight, holding out his hand.

'Deal.' said Sir Trober, taking his hand and shaking it.

The two knights took their horses to either end of the road. 'On three' said the Dark Knight, drawing his long dark sword. The sword looked like it had seen a lot of fighting, but Trober was too angry to be scared now.

'1…2…3!'

They rode towards each other and Trober hit the first blow, bringing his sword down on the Dark Knight's shoulder. But as he heard the clashing of the metal, the Dark Knight brought his sword down on Trober's helmet with a crash.

'Dong!' laughed the Dark Knight.

Furious, and with a sore head, Trober turned his horse around in a circle, before riding back at the Dark Knight again. 'Come on!' yelled the Dark Knight, 'Coward!'

Trober brought his sword against the Knight's other shoulder, trying to push sideways with all his might.

The Dark Knight however lifted his shoulder, ducking under Trober's sword and turned his horse around shouting, 'that was like being pushed by a baby! Are you a knight of the Idrim or not?'

Trober was very angry now. He was so angry, that he charged his horse after the Dark Knight, his sword raised high above his head, and brought it down with a crash on the dented helmet of the other knight.

Or that was what he had planned to do.

What really happened, was that the Dark Knight suddenly stopped his horse, and as Trober's horse continued to gallop past, the Knight stuck out his elbow, knocking Trober sideways off his still moving horse.

Trober lay flat on the ground trying to work out what just happened. The Dark Knight appeared above him, still wearing his helmet, and holding Trober's horse by the reins, 'Here,' he said, 'Keep your horse and your wits about you, and maybe focus more on your eyes and less on your ears, and you might not be such a bad knight after all. Heed well what I've taught you. You probably won't ever see me again if you are lucky.'

Farewell Sir Trober!'

And with that he galloped off down the road, continuing on his journey. Sir Trober shut his eyes and groaned. What a bad day he was having.

But it got worse. When he got back to the castle, he found out that there was going to be a new training tournament among the Knights of the Idrim, where they each jousted with each other, one every day

for the week, and the winners rode against each other the next week.

And again it got worse. For who was Trober to ride against that day but Sir Anni Groeg. 'Hey Trober!' she called from the other side of the room where the list was pinned to a wall. 'See you out there

later! Lucky me, starting off all easy, I'll be finished in no time!'
Trober began to feel angry, but then he remembered what the Dark
Knight had said, and he tried very hard instead to think of all the
moves he could use in the tournament as he left the room to go and
get ready

Later that day, Trober met Anni Groeg at the arena with their horses.
The other knights were all sitting in the spectator stands, ready to
ride their own challenges afterwards. At the front was Sir Ardnax
holding a large bell. 'Ready?' he yelled.

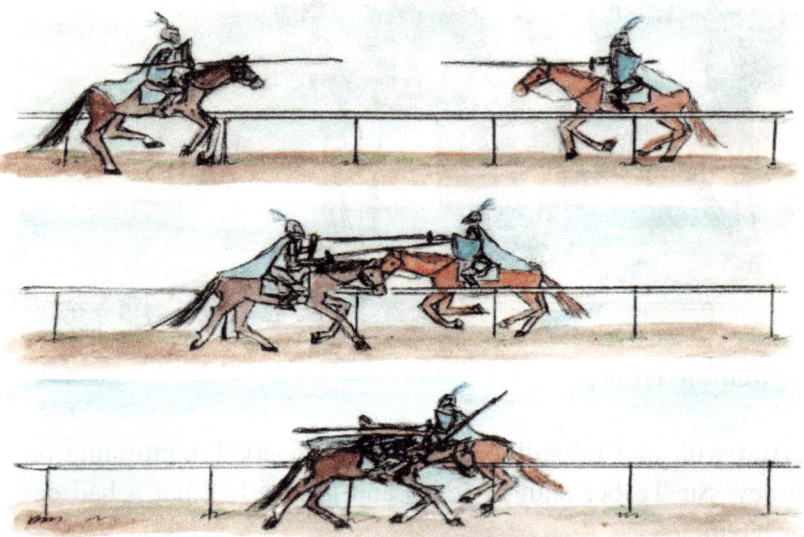

Anni Groeg and Trober moved to opposite ends of the arena, and
hoisted up their lances.
Ardnax rang the bell loudly and the two knights galloped towards
each other, lances at the ready. Trober missed Anni Groeg, but
though she caught his shield, he didn't fall off.

'Nice one Trober!' she yelled as she reached the other end, 'But you
are supposed to try and hit me, not the floor!' A few of the other
knights laughed in the stands. Trober began to feel angry again, and
got ready. 'Use your eyes and less of your ears' he suddenly
remembered. He could see Anni Groeg was shouting something else,
but this time he decided not to listen. Instead he concentrated on
keeping his lance up. Sir Ardnax rang the bell again, and the two

knights charged once more. This time both lances hit the other knights' shield making a horrible screeching sound.

'Trober!' yelled Anni Groeg, 'Well done you broke your record of...one run!'

'Don't listen to her,' said Trober to himself. 'Eyes not ears.'

The third time they rode together. This time Trober ducked low and focused on hitting Anni Groeg with all his strength. The lance slid beside her shield and hit her in the shoulder, knocking her sideways whilst her own lance skimmed over his back. As he rode past he gave one last shove with his elbow as the Dark Knight had done, and then he had ridden past and the moment was over. There was silence.

Trober turned round to see Anni Groeg sitting on the floor!

There came a round of applause from the other knights and much laughter and cheering. 'Well done Trober!' cried out Sir Narf. Even Anni Groeg, though grumpy, pulled herself up and shook Sir Trober's hand with a quiet 'Well done.'

Sir Trober couldn't believe it! It was the first time since he was made one of the Idrim that he had ever got past the first stage of a tournament! And all because of the lesson from the Dark Knight he had met at the crossroads earlier that day.

It was not such a bad day after all.

3. Sir Trober and the Dark Night

One night, after a long day of work chasing a thief around Idris, Sir Trober finally got back to the castle. He put his horse to bed, then climbed the stairs of the knight's quarters to his own bed. However, as he opened the door he heard the sound of paper rustling. It was getting dark and Trober could only just about read the neatly written note that had been slid under his door.

Dear Sir Trober.

Meeting tomorrow, 2.30 till 5.30. We need to talk about the dragons seen in the forest. Don't be late.

Yours sincerely,

Sir Ardnax

Sir Trober thought to himself, 'How exciting!' but then he remembered he had to leave early in the morning to check on the thief he had caught in the castle jail. 'I better write a quick note back,' he said 'in case I have to go before Ardnax is awake.' It was getting darker as Trober went to his desk, and pulled out a sheet of paper. He patted around on his desk trying to find the ink pot that he thought he had left there but was unable to find it in the dark. 'I must light a candle.' he decided, and reached for the candle he kept near his bed. But the candle had melted so low it wouldn't last a few seconds. Trober had kept meaning to get a new one to replace it but always forgot.

He sighed and went to get a new candle from the supply in the main room of the knight's quarters. The corridor to get to the room

from Trober's was very dark, and Trober crept along carefully. He looked out of a window and saw how cloudy it was, there wasn't even any moonlight. 'All the more need for a candle...' whispered Trober to himself, and walked onwards with his hands out in front of him.

'Who goes there?!' came a shout from inside one of the rooms he walked past. 'Why are you sneaking around in the dark at this time of night!?' The voice was Anni Groeg.

'I'm not sneaking!' said Trober, 'I'm going to get a candle.'

'Well you don't have to be so loud about it!' complained Anni Groeg, 'or someone might take you for a thief!'

'Go to sleep' said Sir Trober grumpily.

'I was!' said Anni Groeg, 'till SOMEONE woke me up...'

'Night.' said Trober and carried onwards to the main room, with his hands out in front of him.

It really was very dark now. Unfortunately it was so late at night that the candles in the main room had burned out, and Trober had to fumble around in the dark to find the spares. He knew which cupboard they were in, but not

which of the 4 drawers in side. The last drawer he checked was the right one, he could feel the candle in his hand, and he was just about to turn around and head back to his room, when he suddenly heard a sound from the doorway. Before he could turn around to look, someone hit him hard in the back and he found himself on the floor, with his attacker kneeling on his chest. 'Ouch!' said Trober, too tired for fighting, 'What are you doing?'

'What are YOU doing?' started the attacker, then stopped. 'Wait, Trober is that you?'

There was the sound of a match being lit, and a small flame appeared showing the face of Sir Liw.

'Sorry Trober, what are you doing clattering around in here in the pitch black?'

Trober grumpily explained what he had been trying to do. Liw laughed, 'Oh dear Trober, look I'll tell Ardnax about you having to leave early in the morning, you just get to bed.' He then lit Trober's candle with one of his matches, and vanished back into his room next to the door.

Trober began to head back to his room, very glad for the candle in the now completely dark corridor.

However, just as he turned the last corner, a gust of wind through a window blew his candle right out and yet again, Trober was in the dark. 'Blast!' he whispered to himself, and carefully continued along the corridor.

What Trober hadn't realised was that after being knocked down by Sir Liw he was feeling pretty dizzy and had taken the wrong corridor out of the main room and was going the wrong way!

Just then there was a noise from the room he was passing, which was not Sir Anni Groeg's room as Trober thought. He was about to shout out that it was only him again and to please not attack him but it was too late.

A boot kicked him in the side and before he knew what was

happening Trober tumbled sideways and fell out of the window.

There was good news and bad news about this. The good news was that he had a soft landing. The bad news was that the soft landing was a huge pile of horse poo behind the stables.

'Serves you right intruder!' yelled a voice from the window above where Trober lay. In the light of the candle held by his attacker, he could just about see the bright ginger hair of his friend Narf.

'Narf! Its me!' shouted Trober angrily.

'Trober? Is that you!? Oh no I'm so sorry!' Narf yelled. 'Oh no how could I? Oh Trober I'm so sorry!' He continued to shout loudly about how sorry he was, close to tears, till all the other knights were woken up and came to see what was going on.

First was Anni Groeg, furious at being woken for the second time, followed by Sir Liw and Sir Ardnax who were worried that something terrible had happened. Then came Sir Sej complaining that he needed his beauty sleep, and how selfish they all were for waking him up. Finally came Sir Vic, who on seeing that no serious trouble was taking place, headed to the kitchen for a midnight feast.

Later assembled in the main room, (after Trober had been pulled from the top of the rather high pile of poo!) Ardnax addressed the knights as sternly as he could given that they were all in dressing gowns and pyjamas, except for Trober who was covered head to toe in horse poo!

'Please could you all take this as a lesson to not be creeping around like thieves at night time,' said Sir Ardnax. 'I want you all to remain alert for if we really did have an intruder and false alarms will not help this! Also please don't put off replacing candles in your room till you run out, so that no one will have to be creeping around in the first place. Now, Trober go wash yourself, and everyone else to bed. I don't want to hear any other noises tonight!'

4. Sir Trober and the Black and Red Dragon

Sir Trober and the other knights of the Idrim were all sat round the fire after dinner, discussing dragons. There hadn't been dragons seen in the forests around Idris for many years, but people in the city had been talking about a group that had apparently been seen leaving the mountains and were coming towards the city. Sir Ardnax had even held a meeting about it earlier that day.

'I heard that there is a really fierce green and bronze one,' said Sir Sej, 'who is big enough to eat a horse whole and still have room for more!'

'I heard,' said Sir Vic, his mouth full of cake, 'That there is an even bigger blue one with golden markings, who is the size of a house!'

'Green and blue dragons?' said Sir Anni Groeg, 'Well they sound nothing compared to the black and red dragon!'

'How...how...how big is he?' asked Sir Narf.

'The black and red dragon is the size of this castle!' said Sir Anni Groeg, 'His eyes are the size of wagon wheels and his teeth and claws each the length of a horse. Not to mention his tail, which is as long as a river, and barbed with spikes like swords!'

All the knights looked worriedly at each other, except for one.

'These dragons are nothing to be scared about' said Sir Ardnax boldly. 'We are the Knights of the Idrim! The greatest knights in the land! No dragon scares me.'

Sir Trober listened to all of this, and he was struck by an idea. 'If I could kill the black and red dragon,' he said to himself, 'I would be the greatest knight in the land!'

'What was that Trober?' asked Sir Narf.

'Nothing,' said Sir Trober, 'I think I will go for a short ride tomorrow to hear more about these dragons…'

Early the next morning before training, Sir Trober set off riding through the woods. He galloped along his normal path around the edge of the borders of Idris looking for any evidence of dragons. Sir Trober had never seen a dragon before, but he knew what they looked like from the other knights and thought they shouldn't be hard to find. After an hour he came upon a rock that he didn't recognise. It was large and green with bronze pointy bits on top. Sir Trober was just about to get out a map to see where he had gone wrong on his usual path, when the rock moved! A huge green face the size of two horses lifted up from the ground where it had been resting, and turned one of its huge bronze eyes towards Sir Trober.

'Where are you going young knight?' growled the green dragon. 'Are you here to fight me?'

'No!' Sir Trober squeaked, as he tried to stop his horse from galloping away as fast as it could. 'No I...I'm looking for the black and red dragon.'

'Hmm' growled the dragon, 'Where are you from?'

'The city of Idris, an hour that way,' said Sir Trober in a high voice.

'Good bye then,' said the green dragon, getting up from it's rest to stretch, 'You'll have to keep riding if you are to find the black and red dragon...' And with that he walked off in the opposite direction to Sir Trober, who quickly galloped his horse onwards, and began to wonder if this was such a good idea after all.

After another hour of riding through the woods, Sir Trober felt the ground underneath him shake, and his horse stopped galloping immediately and neighed loudly. Just then the trees in front of them shook, and through them came a huge blue dragon the size of a house with gold markings on his face and back. The dragon saw Sir Trober, and lowered its enormous head to look at him with one huge yellow eye. 'Where are you going young knight?' growled the blue dragon, in a lower voice than the green dragon. 'Are you here to fight me?'

'No!' Sir Trober squeaked. 'No I...I'm looking for the black and red dragon.'

'Hmm,' growled the dragon, 'Where are you from?'

'The city of Idris, 2 hours that way.' said Sir Trober in a high voice.

'Good bye then,' said the blue dragon, 'You'll have to keep riding if you are to find the black and red dragon…' And with that he walked off in the opposite direction to Sir Trober, who quickly galloped his horse onwards, and continued to wonder if this was such a good idea after all.

After a third hour of riding through the woods, the land around Sir Trober suddenly all fell into shadow. Sir Trober looked to the sky to see a large black bird which seemed to be hovering in front of the sun. The bird grew larger, and larger still as it dropped nearer to the ground, till it became clear this was not a bird.

When the black dragon landed in front of Sir Trober, the trees all around were knocked down by the force of his huge wings, and the ground shook so badly that Sir Trober fell off his horse as it fell over and galloped for the trees. The dragon let loose a huge roar, baring its teeth the length of horses and its huge cave like mouth, before swinging around its tail knocking over even more trees with its red spikes like swords. Finally the dragon brought its giant head down to the height of Sir Trober to look at him with one huge red eye the size of a wagon wheel.

'Where are you going young knight?' growled the black dragon, in a lower and louder voice than the green and blue dragons. 'Are you here to fight me?'

'No!' Sir Trober squeaked. 'No I…' He meant to say yes and grab his sword as planned, but he could not do it with the castle size dragon in front of him. The dragon could swallow him whole as Trober would eat a grape, or squish him like Trober would an ant!

'Ha!' growled the dragon and he laughed in a horrible low way. 'Where are you from?'

'The city, 3 hours that way.' said Sir Trober in a high voice.

'Ah,' said the black dragon, raising his head to look far into the

distance. 'That happens to be the city I am heading for. My friends have invited me to attack the city together though they went ahead of me. They said a silly little knight showed them how to get there.'

Sir Trober's mouth dropped wide open.

'In fact I think I'll hurry up and head off there right now,' said the black dragon, 'Else there won't be any houses left for me to burn or any people to eat,' and with that the black dragon lifted its mighty wings, and brought them down again, knocking down even more trees, and lifting itself up high into the clouds as it shot off in the direction of the city.

Sir Trober, once he had caught his breath, quickly got hold of his horse, and started riding back to the city as fast as he possibly could.

It took him two and a half hours, and by the time he got close, he was surprised to not be able to see any dragons in the sky over the city. There were a lot of burned houses, and at first Sir Trober thought the whole city had been eaten by dragons since nobody seemed to be there!

But then he heard the sounds of much cheering and shouting from the castle. There was a great feast of celebration in the castle, which the whole city had been invited to, and the knights were all seated at the head of the feast, receiving much praise and glory from everyone there. Some people were calling them names such as Sir Ardnax the Dragonheart, Sir Narf and Sir Sej the Dragonstabbers, Sir Liw and Sir Vic Dragon's bane, Sir Anni Groeg the Wingworthy, and many more names besides, only some of which were remembered the next day.

Sir Trober walked quietly into the hall hoping no one would see him, but Sir Narf did. 'Sir Trober!' He cried from the head table, 'Where have you been? Come sit here we have so much to tell you!'

A huge battle had been fought between the dragons and the knights of the Idrim. The knights had worked together and bravely managed to protect the city. Though the great bridge and many of the boats in the harbour had been burned down, the city had been evacuated into the castle or to the woods after Sir Liw spotted the dragons from a distance and raised the alarm. Sir Narf and Sir Sej had together managed to kill the green dragon by jumping on to him from the castle roof and stabbing between his scales.

The blue dragon had come next, but after the green one, the knights were prepared and on the lookout. Sir Liw and Sir Vic had managed to hit the beast with a huge rock from the catapults on the city wall, crashing the dragon into the sea.

When the black dragon had arrived, he had been too big to jump onto from the castle, and a rock from the catapults only smashed on his side, like throwing a pea at a man. Sir Anni Groeg however waited till the dragon swept low and then caught hold of a red spike on the dragon's tail as it flew past carrying her up into the air. The dragon swung its tail shaking her off but she landed on the dragon's wing, which she then tore with her sword. The black dragon screamed terribly and fell to the ground crushing five empty houses, pouring out fire all around and shaking the ground with its trampling.

Sir Anni Groeg was knocked out in the crash, and the other knights were all trying to put out the flames to get through. At which point, the brave Sir Ardnax charged through the flames and holding a great long spear, leapt onto the dragon's side, and plunged the spear deep into the dragon, stabbing it in the heart and bringing the battle to an end.

'So where were you?' asked Sir Vic, his mouth full of roast beef.

'Yes where were *you*?' asked Sir Anni Groeg, her hair still burned black from the flames.

'I went for a walk.' said Sir Trober grumpily. 'I went for a walk in the woods.'

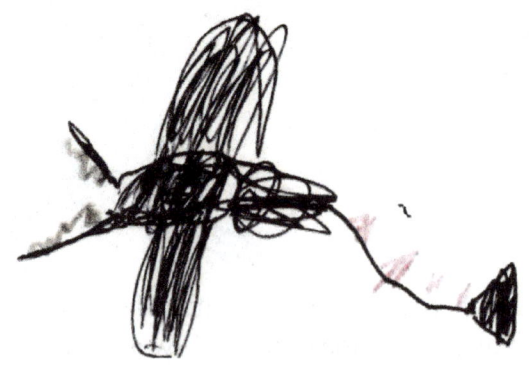

5. Sir Trober the Archer

One day in Idris, the knights were practicing their archery in a field near the castle. Ardnax went first to show the other knights the best way to use a bow and arrow.

The first arrow he shot went right in the middle of the red and blue target. The other knights all clapped. The second arrow he shot split the first arrow down the middle!

Again the knights clapped and Sir Narf cheered. 'Wow!' said Sir Trober, beginning to worry, and hoping he wouldn't be chosen to go next.

'Trober, why don't you go next?' said Sir Ardnax.

'Blast!' thought Sir Trober to

himself, but he lifted up his bow and arrow and stepped forward, to take Sir Ardnax's position.

He carefully aimed at the target, but when he pulled the bow string back, the bow broke!

Everyone looked at him.

'Ummmm must have been broken already by someone else earlier,' said Sir Trober quickly, picking up the pieces, 'Errr I'm going to go fix it now!'

He turned and left the field as quickly as he could whilst still trying to look relaxed. The other knights watched him go, 'Why don't you go next Sir Liw?' Said Sir Ardnax to change the topic.

Trober first went to his room, where he hid the bow under his bed. Then he ran to the stables, saddled up his horse and galloped down the steep hill to the rest of the city.

In the city he bought a really expensive bow from the best weaponry shop in Idris, and then rushed back to the archery training, hoping no one realised how long he had been away.

When he arrived, Sir Vic was just finishing his go. The two arrows he had fired were both very close to the yellow circle in the middle of the target, but not quite as close to the centre as Sir Ardnax and

Sir Liw's. Scattered around the target were arrows from the other knights in the different coloured circles. There was even one arrow that had missed the target completely and was stuck in the grass a few yards away. Trober noticed the orange and green feathers of the arrow, and realised it was probably Sir Narf's. 'Well done Vic,' said Sir Ardnax kindly as Sir Vic put his bow down. 'Keep up the good work!' He turned and saw Trober, who was out of breath from all his rushing around. 'Ah Trober,' he said, 'I see you've fixed your bow. Are you ready for your go now?'

'Of course,' said Sir Trober, trying to sound more confident than he felt.

Taking his place next to Sir Ardnax again, he lifted his bow up, drew back the string, and fired an arrow but it went too high, flying above the target towards the buildings of the Knight's quarters, and when it came down again…it hit Sir Narf's stable door!

Sir Trober's mouth dropped wide open as Narf's horse neighed angrily. 'Sorry,' said Trober quickly, and lifted his bow again for another go.

This time when he fired the arrow, it didn't go far enough, and came down right next to Sir Anni Groeg's foot.

Anni Groeg jumped sideways at first, and then laughed. 'HA!' she said, 'The target's THAT way Trober!" and she laughed again.

'Anni Groeg!' said Sir Ardnax warningly.

Sir Trober was very fed up with his new bow. It was meant to be a good one!

'I nearly hit you on purpose scardeycat!' he said angrily to Anni Groeg.

'Trober!' said Sir Ardnax sternly.

But Sir Trober stomped away out of the training ground and through the gate in the castle wall, and kept walking and walking till he reached the forest. He was feeling very tired and miserable so soon he stopped and sat down under a tree. Suddenly he noticed a stick on the ground nearby which looked a bit like a bow, and it gave him a thought.

He took the stick back to the castle and found some bowstring. He tied this to either end of the stick and it looked and felt so much like a good real bow that he took it back to the archery practice, which was just finishing.

'Come on Trober!' shouted Narf, who was just picking up his green and orange feathered arrows from the grass, 'We're off to dinner now!'

'Beef tonight!!' added Sir Vic, 'My favourite, I hope there's pudding too!' and he jogged off quickly in the direction of the kitchens.

Trober ignored both of them, and as the other knights were leaving, he lifted his newly made bow up and aimed at the target.

Some of the other knights stopped to watch. 'Go on Trober!' said Ardnax, 'One last shot for the night. Chin up!'

'A little higher' said Sir Liw.

'Aim for the target!' said Sir Anni Groeg, trying to be helpful for once, but not being very helpful at all.

Sir Trober did all the things they told him to; he lifted his chin, aimed a little higher at the target, pulled back his bowstring and fired the arrow…

It hit the target right in the middle!

All the knights cheered. Sir Trober was amazed, he couldn't believe it!

He shot again. This time the arrow hit the ground in front of him. The other knights all went quiet.

DINNERTIME!' yelled Sir Vic from the distance

6. Sir Trober and the Mysterious lights

Once upon a time, Sir Trober of the Idrim went out riding in the dark woods. None of the knights were supposed to go out riding in the dark woods alone, for there were many strange stories about the woods, and those who lived there, but Sir Trober wasn't scared of

any strange stories, or so he had said to Sir Anni Groeg that morning.

'You are not brave,' she had said, 'You ran away that day that the dragons came!'

'I went for a walk in the woods!' Sir Trober had said, 'I didn't know the dragons would come!'

'Yeah yeah yeah,' said Sir Anni Groeg.

'I'll show you,' Sir Trober said, 'Today I will go out riding in the dark woods, all by myself!'

As he was galloping through the dark trees, trying not to think about strange stories, he suddenly caught a glimpse of a bright light. Bringing his horse to a stop, Sir Trober looked through the trees and what he saw made his mouth drop wide open. Floating in the darkness beneath the branches of a huge old tree, was a circle of seven bright round balls of light. They were so pretty, that Sir Trober began to ride towards them. He stopped, wondering whether he should wait for one of the other knights first, but then he thought of how brave everyone would think he was if he brought back one of the lights for the city. He could show it off in front of all the other knights and the look on Sir Anni Groeg's face when he proved her wrong…

He carried on towards the strange mysterious lights.

He reached out to grab one from the air, but as he touched the light, he suddenly vanished from the clearing.

Now, all of the other knights were back at the castle having lunch, and some were beginning to worry about Sir Trober. 'What if he has been eaten by a werewolf?' said Sir Vic, with his mouth full of bread.

'Or been turned into a frog by a witch!' said Sir Narf.

'I'm not going after him till four o'clock,' said Sir Anni Groeg stubbornly. 'If he wants to show how brave he is, then it's his fault if he gets himself into trouble.'

Sir Vic and Sir Narf however, were very worried. Finally, at two o'clock, they decided to ride into the dark woods together to look for Sir Trober. As they rode on by, they were very scared because of the strange stories they had heard of the dark wood, but they kept on riding between the tall dark trees till they also came to the ring of mysterious lights.

'Sir Narf look!' cried out Sir Vic, a chunk of apple falling out of his mouth in surprise.

'They are so pretty,' said Sir Narf. 'I wonder…'

They both thought about how great it would be to bring a light home. They both looked at each other. Then charged, each one trying to grab a light before the other one. They reached the circle of light at the same time, and as they each touched a glowing ball, they too vanished from the clearing.

34

Finally four o'clock came around, and Sir Anni Groeg was beginning to worry about the other knights. Something must be wrong for Sir Vic to miss tea time. Anni Groeg was not scared of the dark woods at all. If Sir Trober could go, so could she, and so she galloped off through the dark woods all by herself. When she came to the circle of lights, she saw that there must be some magic at work as she had expected. Instead of staring at the circle of lights, she rode around the clearing, looking at the trees. Suddenly she realised that tied to each of the trees, hidden by the darkness, were each of the three knights who had vanished. All of them were awake but had scarves over their mouths, their hands and feet tied up so they could not make a sound. Sir Anni Groeg hopped off her horse to cut them loose, but just then the lights turned brighter, and a loud low voice from the dark said,

'To free your friends, you must first fight me.'

'Who are you Sir?' called Sir Anni Groeg, 'and where are you?'

'To free your friends, you must first fight me.' Repeated the voice,

'However, your friends can help you or you can fight me alone. What do you wish?'

'I don't need their help,' said Sir Anni Groeg. 'I'll fight you by myself.' She drew her sword.

As soon as she spoke, the circle of seven lights all broke from the circle and flew at her. She tried to hit them with her sword. She managed to hit two, but there were too many for one person, and soon one hit her on the head and she vanished from the clearing.

Back at the castle, Sir Ardnax was walking down to the knight's room, after a very important meeting with the Lady of Idris about some building work needed to fix the houses the dragons had broken. As he entered the room, he was surprised to see that only Sir Liw and Sir Sej were at the table.

'Where are the others?' he asked.

Sir Lim laughed, 'They have all gone to the dark woods, one by one' he said, holding up a note left by Sir Anni Groeg, 'Sir Trober started it, and they have all gone looking for him!'

Sir Ardnax sighed, 'Well we better go and find them then.'

They galloped through the dark woods, Sir Ardnax at the front, with Sir Lim and Sir Sej just behind.

Soon they too came to the circle of seven bright lights. Sir Lim and Sir Sej began to move towards the lights but Sir Ardnax held out his sword to stop them going any further. 'Look at the trees' he said.

There were now four knights tied to the trees around the lights; Sir Anni Groeg, Sir Trober, Sir Vic and Sir Narf, and none of them looked very happy.

The voice spoke again. 'To free your friends, you must first fight me.'

'Who are you?' asked Sir Ardnax, 'And why have you tied up my knights?'

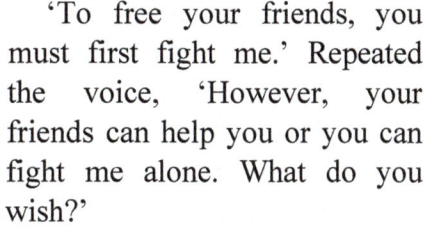

'To free your friends, you must first fight me.' Repeated the voice, 'However, your friends can help you or you can fight me alone. What do you wish?'

Sir Ardnax frowned, 'I wish for all of my knights to fight together. Many hands make light work.'

As soon as he spoke, the ropes vanished from the tied up knights, and the lights from the circle all flew at them. One light for each knight.

Sir Ardnax stabbed his with one blow, and the light flared up and dropped to the ground as a small white stone. The other knights took a little longer, hitting the lights away again and again. The last to stab his light was Sir Trober. A silence fell on the dark wood.

'I hope you have all learned a lesson today,' said Sir Ardnax sternly, 'or maybe two or three lessons?' he looked at Sir Trober.

'We knights are here to protect our city, not to hunt for glory. Understood?'

All the knights nodded glumly.

'We are a team and we fight together,' continued Sir Ardnax, 'Alone we are just knights, but together we are the Idrim and we can achieve great things IF we work together. Understood?'
Again all the knights nodded.

'Right then,' sighed Sir Ardnax. 'Back to the castle, we have important things to discuss from my meeting with the Lady of Idris, and you two!' he pointed at Sir Trober and Sir Anni Groeg, 'Don't you even think about arguing! I don't care who started it, your arguments have brought us here and wasted a whole day. If you don't have anything nice or helpful to say to each other, don't say it at all!'

And with that, Sir Ardnax turned and galloped back to the castle. The other knights all followed. Sir Trober and Sir Anni Groeg looked at each other. 'You have a leaf in your hair,' said Sir Anni Groeg very grumpily.

'Thanks,' said Sir Trober even more grumpily.

7. Sir Trober and the King's Visit

There was a lot of excitement in the city of Idris. The King was coming to visit!

The seamstresses were busy making lots of banners to hang from the houses, and children were sent to hang bunting all along the main street from the harbour to the castle, to decorate the way the King would ride through the city. The cooks were busy baking and the cleaners scrubbing, all working their hardest to make the castle as welcoming as possible to the King. There was going to be a huge feast with lots of dancing and music and everyone was invited!

The Knights of the Idrim were busy as well. It was their job to meet the King at the castle gates, and there was a lot to do to get ready. Horses had to be cleaned and groomed to look their best, saddles had to be scrubbed and shiny, armour had to be polished and The Knights themselves had to look clean.

The afternoon of the day before the King came, Anni Groeg and Trober were on patrol duty in the woods. The last two days had been very rainy and when they came into the stables at the end of their ride, there was a lot of mud everywhere. Trober put his horse away and headed out back to the castle.

'Aren't you going to clean your horse?' said Sir Anni Groeg from where she was giving her horse a good brush down.

'I will,' said Trober, 'I'm just going to go and have a sit down first, I'm pretty tired.'

'You could clean your horse first.' said Anni Groeg.

'I'll do it afterwards!' said Trober angrily, and walked out of the stables.

On his way into the castle he walked through the tack room. Sir Narf was sitting in the room, scrubbing so hard at his saddle that his knuckles had gone white. 'Hello Trober,' said Narf, 'Are you going to scrub your saddle for tomorrow?'

'In a bit,' said Trober, 'I've just got to go and have a sit down first.'

'You could sit down and polish your saddle at the same time...' said Narf.

'I will in a bit!' said Trober.

Trober left Narf cleaning his saddle, and went to take his armour off in the armoury. He found Sir Vic polishing his armour, and Sir Liw polishing his long sword. 'Hello Trober,' said Vic, who was chewing on a biscuit. 'Come to clean your armour with us?'

'No, I'm going to do it later,' said Trober, 'I'm just going to have a rest first.'

'You could come and sit with us and do it now,' said Liw, 'Then you won't have to do it later,'

'And we have biscuits!' added Sir Vic.

'I'm going to do it later!' said Trober, and walked out of the room, leaving his dirty armour on its peg.

On his way to his bedroom, Sir Trober walked through the main room of the Knight's quarters. Sir Ardnax was sitting at his desk, writing out the plans for the next day. 'Are you ready for tomorrow Trober?' said Ardnax.

'Nearly,' said Trober, 'I've got a few things to do later, I'm just going to my room first.'

'Well don't leave it too late.' said Ardnax, before turning back to his important plans.

Trober was walking down the corridor to his room, when Sej came out of the bathroom in his towel, his hair still wet from his bath.

'All ready for tomorrow?' he said cheerfully to Trober. 'I finished all my cleaning earlier so just had a good wash myself, is that why you're here?'

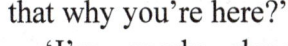

'I'm nearly done,' said Trober, feeling very grumpy, and wrinkling his nose at the smell of Sej's soap. 'Just a few things to do…'

'Ah well,' said Sej, walking to his room, taking his soapy smell with him, 'See you later, oh and by the way, it's supposed to be quite cold tonight, so make sure you put your horse's rug on so that he can have a good night's sleep before tomorrow.'

'I will,' said Trober, starting to worry about the number of things he had to do. 'See you later.'

Trober lay down on his bed thinking he would have a quick half an hour nap. He opened his eyes. The clock on the wall said seven o' clock. It had been three hours! It couldn't have been, thought Trober, I only shut my eyes for a second. He ran down stairs and checked all the other

clocks. It was true. It was seven o' clock in the evening and he had a lot to do! All the other knights were going into the dinner hall as Trober rushed past to the stables.

'Trober where are you going?' called Vic. 'It's dinner time!' But Trober didn't listen.

Hurriedly he brushed his horse to try and get all the mud off but it was too dark in the stables to be sure he had got every speck of dirt. Then he rushed to the tack room to clean his saddle, in his hurry forgetting to add the soap to the scrubbing brush. Next he ran to the armoury and polished his armour, but kept forgetting which bit he had done, and trying to be quick he got so confused. Finally he rushed back to the knight's quarters forgetting to clean his sword and tried to have a bath.

But all the castle servants had gone to bed so he couldn't get any hot water because the fires had all been put out, and he didn't have time. So he tried to wash his hair in the cold water, with much spluttering and splashing before finally falling into bed. He fell asleep straight away, unlike his horse who couldn't sleep at all that night because it was a cold night and Trober had forgotten to put his rug on.

The next morning came round very quickly. The knights all got ready very quickly and rushed down to the stables. Trober realised as he put on his armour, he had forgotten to polish his left leg armour, and the back of his helmet, but he hoped no one would notice. He also hoped there was no reason to pull his sword out, because when he tried, it was all sticky and wouldn't come out of its scabbard without a very strong pull. His saddle wasn't as shiny as the other knights, and he suddenly remembered why. He had a horrible shock when he looked in a window on the way to the stable and realised his hair was all sticking out like a cloud around his head. He quickly put his helmet on to hide it. Finally all The Knights reached the stables and saddled up before riding out of the front of the castle to stand in front of the gate. It was eight o' clock in the morning, and the King was due anytime between eight o' clock and ten o' clock depending on how quickly his boat reached the harbour. The Knights had to keep their horses standing smartly in a straight line till the King got there.

Sir Ardnax was first in the line on his great bright bay stallion. Next along was Sir Liw on his dark bay horse which was standing as still as a statue. Beside Liw was Sir Sej on his golden horse. A sweet soap smell surrounded him, and his hair was neatly curled. Next was Sir Anni Groeg on her chestnut horse. The horse's coat was gleaming as bronze as the horse on her shield from its good clean the day before. Beside Anni Groeg was Sir Vic on his rather chubby dapple grey. Vic was chewing a sneaky biscuit, and his horse was chewing some grass. Second to last in the line was Sir Narf on his roan who looked dirty despite the good clean Narf had given him but his orange and green shield was shining so bright it could be seen all the way from the harbour. Finally there was Sir Trober, who was the only knight still wearing his helmet (to try and hide his hair). His bay horse had a patch of mud on its back that he had missed the night before, and looked like it was about to fall asleep at any moment. The Knights stood waiting, trying to keep their horses in line.

Suddenly a shout went up from the harbour- The King's boat had arrived!

'Get ready everyone!' said Sir Ardnax, 'They will be here soon!'

The King came riding up the hill in a grand carriage, followed by people from the city who were throwing confetti and flowers and cheering.

The Lady of Idris walked out to meet the King, and bowed as he got out of the carriage. 'Your majesty,' she said, 'Welcome to Idris, we are most honoured to have you here.'

'Thank you,' said the King. 'I see your Idrim have all lined up to greet me, I must meet them all'

'They would be honoured.' said the Lady, giving The Knights a worried look.

The King walked first, over to Ardnax. 'Sir Ardnax.' said the King nodding.

'Your majesty,' said Sir Ardnax, 'It is an honour to meet you again, let me introduce you to my knights.'

'First, my second in command, Sir Liw.' Sir Liw and his horse moved for the first time in two hours, giving the King a polite nod.

'This is Sir Sej.' continued Ardnax, 'One of our great upcoming knights.' Sir Sej gave a dashing smile as he nodded to the King.

'Sir Anni Groeg has also shown great promise.' said Sir Ardnax. Anni Groeg nodded solemnly, keeping her horse in check.

'This is Sir Vic,' said Ardnax, but before he could add anything else, Sir Vic's horse suddenly made a huge lunge to bite some grass from under the King's feet. Sir Vic quickly pulled the horse's head back up, 'Sorry, sorry, sorry,' he muttered, nodding at the King who didn't look very impressed. The Lady of Idris, who was standing behind the King began to get more nervous.

Ardnax cleared his throat,

'Next we have Sir Narf,' said Ardnax, 'Our youngest...knight.' Ardnax stuttered as in a horrible turn of events, Narf's horse lifted its tail and began to poo! Narf nodded politely at the King before realising what was happening and yanking at his horse's reins, but there was nothing he could do. The smell of horse poo filled the air, and the King did not look very happy.

'Um,' Ardnax paused, angry at his Knights but trying to stay calm, 'And finally, Sir Tro-,' But as Sir Ardnax was saying Trober's name, Trober's horse finally fell asleep, crashing sideways to the floor with a loud clang! There was a loud clatter along the line, as Anni Groeg's horse went to bite the ears of Trober's horse trying to wake him up and Trober yelled at his horse but there was nothing they could do. His horse refused to get up. The King looked very confused and unimpressed. He was quickly ushered away by the Lady of Idris to the castle, leaving a scene of chaos behind that reached a new level of madness when Trober realised he had fallen into Sir's Narf's horse's poo!

Later on that evening, whilst the rest of the city were all at the great feast with the King. The Knights of the Idrim sat in their quarters.

Ardnax had told them to wait there for him, whilst he went to talk with the Lady of Idris.

'It's all your fault,' said Anni Groeg to Trober, 'If you had put your horse's rug on when you were told to.'

Even though Trober knew Anni Groeg was right, he didn't say so.

'It's not my fault Narf's horse-'

'Don't blame me!' said Narf. 'It's not my fault Vic's horse is a pig!'

'Be quiet!' said Sej. 'It's definitely NOT my fault, and I'm fed up of hearing you argue.'

The room fell quiet. Ardnax came through the door with a very serious face.

'Sej and Liw, you can go to the feast.' he said.

'Thank you Sir,' the two knights said and left quickly, hoping to catch some of the good food and dancing. Vic nearly cried.

'Now you four,' said Ardnax sternly, 'are to practice keeping control of your horses every morning for an hour, for the next month, till you can stand in a line and behave.'

'Yes Sir.' they all said miserably.

'And that's not all,' continued Sir Ardnax, 'Narf you are on stable mucking out duty for the next week, Vic you are going on a diet, and Trober is going to clean everyone's horses as soon as they come in from riding for the next month, and no delaying till later!'

'And what about me Sir?' said Anni Groeg.

'You are going to help Sir Trober.'

'No!'

'My word is final,' said Sir Ardnax. 'Narf you need to grow up, Vic you need to be less greedy, Trober you need to learn to do things when you need to, and Anni Groeg you need to learn to get along with Trober!'

Finally Ardnax let the last four knights go to join the feast. Most of the food was gone, and most of the city had gone home. They ate a little bit of what was left before going to bed feeling very miserable. As Trober got out of his clothes he dumped them on the floor thinking

'I'll put them away later.'

Then he paused. There were quite a lot of clothes on the floor. Sighing he bent down and picked them all up again and put them all away in the right places, before finally getting into bed.

THE END

Dear Reader,

First of all, thank you for reading our book!

My little brother Robbie and I started telling each other Trober stories last summer. What began as inventing character names by reversing the letters of our names (with a few alterations!), soon became us taking it in turns to write down and draw our favourite adventures. We hope you enjoyed reading them as much as we enjoyed writing them.

If you did enjoy these tales, we have many more adventures of the Knights of the Idrim which we are looking forward to tell!

Best wishes,

Georgie and Robbie

P.S. Our full names are Georgina and Robert but we think they make much better names backwards...

Lightning Source UK Ltd.
Milton Keynes UK
UKOW07f2051251117
313219UK00009B/83/P